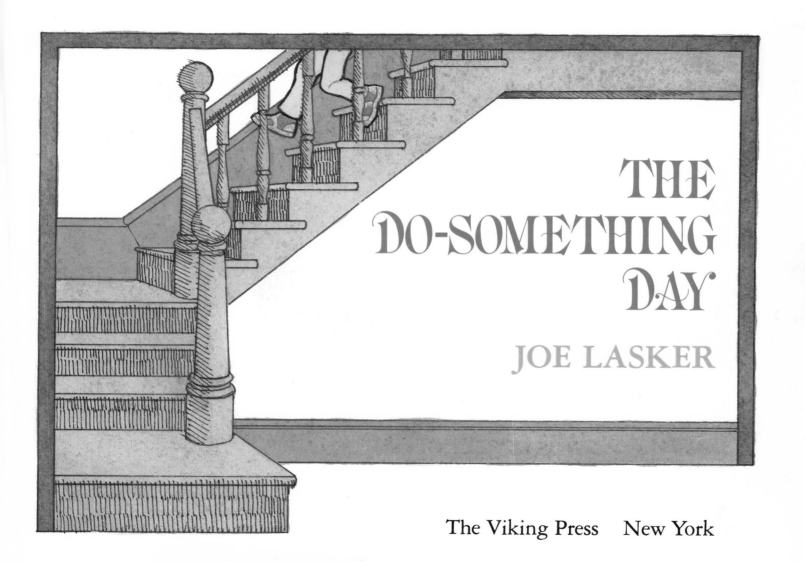

THE DO-SOMETHING DAY

JOE LASKER

The Viking Press   New York

To Antoinette Kraushaar

First Edition · Copyright © Joe Lasker, 1982 · All rights reserved
First published in 1982 by The Viking Press, 625 Madison Avenue, New York, N.Y. 10022
Published simultaneously in Canada by Penguin Books Canada Limited
Printed in U.S.A.   1   2   3   4   5   86   85   84   83   82

Library of Congress Cataloging in Publication Data
Lasker, Joe.   The do-something day.
Summary: While running away from home because no one seems to need his help
for anything, Bernie finds a lot of people on the way who find his help very useful.
[1. Runaways—Fiction. 2. Helpfulness—Fiction. 3. Family life—Fiction] I. Title.
PZ7.L3272Do [E]   81-2508   ISBN 0-670-27503-4   AACR2

Bernie wanted to help. It was a sparkling, sunny, do-something day.
His father said, "Not now, Bernie. I've got to make these plans for tomorrow."

His mother said, "Not now, Bernie. I have to finish these signs for tomorrow."

His brother said, "Not now, Bernie. I'm working on my costume for tomorrow."

Bernie got mad. "No one needs me. I'll run away!"

He left the house and went down the street.

On the way he passed Carl's Garage. "Hello, Bernie," said Carl from under a car. "Where are you going in such a hurry?"

"I'm running away," replied Bernie. "No one wants my help. No one needs me."

"I need your help," said Carl, still under the car.
"Please tell me when these headlights go on and off."

As Carl worked wires and buttons, Bernie said, "Now the lights go on. Now the lights go off."

Carl crawled out and stood up. "Thank you for helping me fix the car, Bernie. So you'll know where you're running to, here's a great big folded road map."

Bernie walked on with his great big folded road map.
Farther up the street he came to Dimple's Delicatessen.

Mr. Dimple was standing in his window, hanging up salamis.

"Hello, Bernie," he said. "Where are you going in such a hurry?"

"I'm running away," replied Bernie. "No one wants my help. No one needs me."

"I need your help," said Mr. Dimple. "Please hand me those salamis." When all the salamis had been hung up, Mr. Dimple climbed down out of the window.

"Thank you for helping me, Bernie. Here's a nice salami and a sour pickle to eat on the way."

So Bernie walked on with his great big folded road map and his nice salami and sour pickle. One block farther on he came to Bertha's Bakery.

Bernie liked Bertha's Bakery because it smelled of fresh baked bread and cookies. Bernie went inside. "I came to say good-bye, Bertha. I'm running away. No one wants my help. No one needs me."

"I need your help," said Bertha. "Please stamp the date on these paper bags. Then stack them on the shelf." Bernie stamped and stamped and stacked and stacked. When he had finished, Bertha said, "Thank you for helping me. Here's a warm rye bread to go with your nice salami and some cookies for dessert."

So Bernie walked on with his great big folded road map, his nice salami and sour pickle and his warm rye bread and cookies. Turning left one block, he came to Pfeffer's Fresh Produce. "Hello, Bernie," said Mr. Pfeffer. "Where are you going in such a hurry?"

"I'm running away," replied Bernie. "No one wants my help. No one needs me."

"I need your help," said Mr. Pfeffer. "Please fetch water for my thirsty horse." He handed Bernie a pail. Bernie took it and filled it at Carl's Garage.

The horse swished its tail from side to side. "My horse Orson thanks you and I thank you," said Mr. Pfeffer. "You'll get thirsty on the road. Here are four purple plums and a bunch of green grapes."

So Bernie walked on with his great big folded road map, his nice salami and sour pickle, his warm rye bread and cookies, and his four purple plums and bunch of green grapes. Turning one block left and one block right, he passed Tom's Shoe Repair. Tom tapped on his window and motioned to Bernie to come in. "Where are you going in such a hurry?" asked Tom.

"I'm running away," replied Bernie. "No one wants my help. No one needs me."

"I need your help," said Tom. "Please deliver this pair of shoes to Bertha the baker."

When Bernie returned from his errand, Tom said, "Thank you, Bernie. Here's a pair of high button shoes. They're out of style, but they'll keep your feet warm when it's cold on the road."

So Bernie walked on with his great big folded road map, his nice salami and sour pickle, his warm rye bread and cookies, his four purple plums and bunch of green grapes, and his pair of high button shoes.

Two blocks farther on was Byrd's Pet Shop. Bernie went
inside. "I came to say good-bye, Mrs. Byrd. I'm running away.
No one wants my help. No one needs me."

"I need your help," said Mrs. Byrd. "Please feed the fish and birds while I feed the puppies and kittens." So Bernie went from tank to tank feeding fish. Then he went from cage to cage feeding the birds. After all the pets had been fed, Mrs. Byrd said, "My fish thank you, my birds thank you, and I thank you.

"You always wanted a dog. Here's another runaway. He's looking for a home and wandered in here. But he's a mutt so I can't sell him. He'll protect you on the road."

"I'll name my mutt Mutt," Bernie said.

So Bernie walked on with his great big folded road map, his nice salami
and sour pickle, his warm rye bread and cookies, his four purple plums
and bunch of green grapes, his pair of high button shoes, and his mutt named
Mutt. He walked on and on and a little farther on until he was so tired
he sat down to rest.

Meanwhile the golden sun was sinking lower in the sky. Long shadows crept across the street and up the sides of houses. The do-something day was coming to an end. Soon it would be dark.

They all needed me and wanted my help, thought Bernie with satisfaction. He looked at his things and had an idea. He got up and started walking home.

His mother, father, and brother were on the porch waiting for him. Slowly he walked up the steps and said, "I ran away."

They looked at him. "Where did you get all those things?"

"On the way when I was running away I said good-bye to Carl the garage man, Mr. Dimple, Bertha the baker, Mr. Pfeffer, Tom the shoemaker, and Mrs. Byrd. They all needed my help and gave me these things."

Bernie gave the road map to his father, who said, "Just what I needed to help me finish the plans for the big fair tomorrow."

Bernie gave the high button shoes to his brother, who said, "Am I in luck! Just what I needed to complete my costume for the big fair pageant."

The four purple plums, the bunch of green grapes, the nice salami and sour
pickle, and the warm rye bread and cookies Bernie gave to his mother. "You're so
helpful, Bernie. Just what we needed to round out our picnic meal at tomorrow's fair."

Then Bernie's father picked up Mutt. "You need Bernie and Bernie
needs you, especially when we get too busy."

His mother smiled. "We need help from one another,
Bernie. But we really need you to love." And she gave him
a great big hug.

Georgetown Elementary School
Indian Prairie School District
Aurora, Illinois

TITLE I MATERIALS

PATRIOTIC PALS

TAILS OF CIVIL WAR DOGS

Chris Stuckenschneider
Art by Richard Bernal

REEDY PRESS

St. Louis, Missouri

Thrilled to the bone to meet you!

The name is Charles Reed Catchaball, but my friends call me Chuck. This is my poodle pal, Tilly, *what a dilly*. She's hounding me to tell you about a road trip we just took. It was a pooch-positive quest to learn about dog heroes from the Civil War.

Our trek began in St. Louis, Missouri, and traveled a route as crooked as a dog's hind leg. Tilly is as proud and primed as a Pointer to tell you about it. Hit the road with us to find out more.

Bless my Beagles.

At the Missouri History Museum in St. Louis there is a dog portrait in oil behind glass, *what a gas*. Sergeant Dick was a stocky mascot with the St. Louis Greys, a militia that kept order, like today's National Guard.

Sarge marched in parades and did double-time with the troops. He also witnessed an early skirmish in the Civil War at Camp Jackson, a bone's throw away from the museum.

Sarge high-stepped himself into our hearts. We had no idea that dogs were so active in the Civil War. Soon we were muzzle deep in research.

Before Tilly could whistle "Dixie," we had a collection of legends about dog mascots that left their paw prints on the hearts of Confederate and Union soldiers.

U.S. CIVIL WAR

April 12, 1861–
May 9, 1865

The Civil War was fought between the Union and the Confederacy. The Union consisted of the Northern states, and the Confederacy was the Southern states.

Tilly's French accent picked up a twitter of twang in Tennessee.

We crossed the state line, and she had to have a moon pie and sweet tea.

The mood got serious when we pulled into Shiloh National Military Park. Many men sacrificed their lives at the Battle of Shiloh, and a dog named Shanks led a heartbroken wife to her fallen soldier.

When Lieutenant Louis Pfieff left home to fight with the Union, Shanks traveled with him from Illinois to Tennessee. Shanks was brave, but he wasn't handsome by any stretch of the Dachshund. Speckled as a Plymouth Rock Rooster, the hound ran with a lumbering lope, from being rammed in the ribs by a sow with a sour attitude.

Shanks had a hero's heart. As the Battle of Shiloh raged, he charged into the fight with his master. Tragically, Lieutenant Pfieff fell and was buried in an unmarked grave.

BATTLE OF SHILOH

April 6-7, 1862

Unionists named the battle after a little white church that became a hospital for the wounded.

Loyal to the end, Shanks stood watch by the grave for 12 days, honoring his lost friend. When Mrs. Pfieff came to Shiloh to find her husband's body, Shanks led her to the lieutenant's grave. Together they took their loved one home.

Shanks

Tilly topped her tail with a scarlet bow in Virginia. Oh, heck. O'Hara! That was taking the Southern belle bit too far in my book.

In Lexington, we visited the home of Confederate General Thomas "Stonewall" Jackson. After the loss at Shiloh, the South needed a lift like a Lab with laryngitis. Stonewall Jackson provided victories in the Shenandoah Valley.

The general was so popular that a company of Confederate soldiers, the Richmond Howitzers, named their mascot in honor of their brave leader. *And that's no woof!*

Stonewall

Stonewall Jackson was a spotted terrier, as brave as his namesake.

Ruff and ready, the snapping spitfire was eager for action on the front lines.

The men grew attached to Stonewall. They were so concerned for the dog's safety that in the heat of battle they stashed him in an ammunition case to keep him safe.

The dog was really keen on Sergeant John Van Lew McCreery. The crafty man made a wooden pipe for the pooch to hold in his mouth during roll call. They didn't know back then that smoking is bad for everyone—even dogs.

FIRST BATTLE OF BULL RUN

July 21, 1861
General Jackson got his nickname at the First Battle of Bull Run, where a fellow soldier said he "stood like a stone wall," opposing the Union.

The plan was to get to Antietam National Battlefield early in the day. Tilly spent hours drumming the pronunciation into my head,

"An-TEE-tum,

An-TEE-tum,

An-TEE-tum."

We finally arrived at the site outside Sharpsburg, Maryland, where one of the biggest battles in the Civil War took place on September 17, 1862. At Antietam, big Brutus stood out. A Newfoundland of epic proportion, Brutus tipped the scale at 130 pounds-plus.

The big guy with grit belonged to the Union's Iron Brigade, specifically to Captain Werner von Bachelle. Entertaining stories about Brutus abound. The dog even learned how to salute, hefting a webbed paw to his face.

Brutus kept the captain on his toes. Legend has it the pooch tried to catch Minie balls in his mouth. Not too smart! Minie balls were a type of bullet. If Brutus had wrapped his mouth around one, it would have been the last thing he chomped down on!

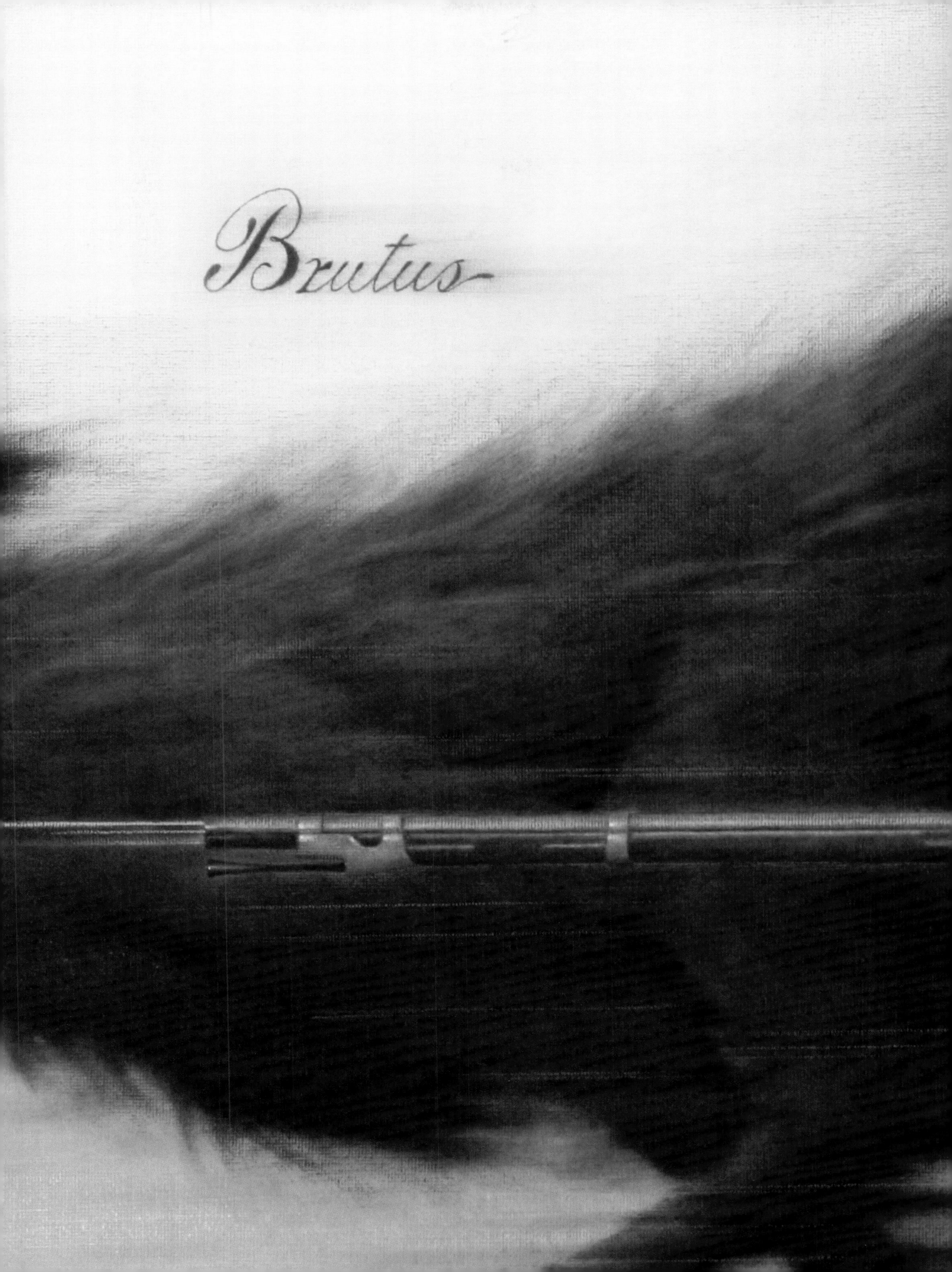
Brutus

Pennsylvania is full of rich American history. It also boasts the town of Hershey. Tilly tried to tempt me with a Kiss or two, but I turned tail on temptation.

It took a crate of canine charm to convince her that chocolate, while tasty, is belly-up bad for dogs.

Pennsylvania is where Gettysburg, the most famous Civil War battle site, is located. The 11th Pennsylvania Volunteer Infantry is honored there with a statue. Sallie, a beloved Brindle Bull Terrier, is memorialized at the base of the monument.

The men got Sallie as a pup.

She was a roly-poly, feisty fighter who
cut her milk teeth on a saber. Sallie
was a girl ahead of her times,
a born and bred soldier.

She braved battles at Antietam,
Fredericksburg, and Chancellorsville.
Wounded twice, Sallie came back for more.

At Gettysburg, President Lincoln
acknowledged her with a military
salute. A heroine for the ages,
Sallie's end came at the Siege
of Petersburg, Virginia, in 1865.

BATTLE OF GETTYSBURG

July 1-3, 1863
Lincoln's famed Gettysburg Address,
delivered at the dedication of the
cemetery, was only 269 words long and
was delivered in just over two minutes.

Our next stop was Ohio.

It was a long haul, but we yapped on about Harvey. He was a bulldog with the 104th Ohio, a rough and tumble bunch of Union soldiers known as the "Barking Dog Regiment." The men were top dogs in the Battle of Franklin, Tennessee.

Tilly made a grand discovery at the Massillon Museum in Ohio. The regiment loved its bullie so much it had pins made with his portrait on the front. Tilly couldn't wait to "pin me!"

HARVEY'S COLLAR

Harvey wore a silver collar inscribed, "I'm Lt. Stearn's dog. Whose dog are you?" Lieutenant Stearn was an officer in the Barking Dog Regiment.

Harvey was a military mutt for sure.

The brave dog took a hit in the Civil War and was taken prisoner. He was returned when a flag of truce was raised.

A real favorite in the camp, Harvey was part of the regiment's menagerie: three dogs, two raccoons, and two squirrels. Harvey didn't take too kindly to having his ear nibbled on by a squirrel. But later he rescued the varmint from another pup's snapping jaws.

All that squirrel talk
made Tilly
crave rodent
on rye, a
hankering
that passed
with a wad of
Double Bubble.

Harvey

L eave it up to Tilly to spring for a stop in Illinois, the Land of Lincoln. The state was home to a tall gent in a stovepipe hat, our nation's 16th president, elected just before the outbreak of the Civil War.

Tilly talked me into swinging by the Abraham Lincoln Presidential Library and Museum in Springfield.

I ate humble pie when I found out Lincoln had a dog named Fido, and I treated Tilly to a slab of Apple Pie à la Mode. Any way you slice it, Springfield was a smart stop.

Fido was Lincoln's family
pet in Springfield.

The dog had a place at the dinner table and used
a horsehair couch as a bed.

When Lincoln won the election, he moved to
the White House in Washington, D.C. Lincoln
found a home for Fido in Springfield with one of
his friends. The horsehair couch went with the
pampered pup, a pooch as spoiled as a lump of
Limburger cheese left out on a dog day in August.

Four years later, after Lincoln was shot, his body
was brought back to Springfield for burial. Trusty
Fido met the train, greeting mourners gathered to
grieve their fallen president.

Fido

Whee doggies—road trips are fun, and rewarding, even if the cupboard is bare when you get back home. Where is Old Mother Hubbard when you need her?

Before Tilly and I hit our sunspots on the porch, we would like to leave you with a bit of kibble to consider. Remember that history is fickle. Facts get altered as tales are passed down from one generation to the next.

Some of the details in our travelogue may be hazy, lots of "as legends have it," but the men's feelings for their canine mascots remain crystal clear.

In the Civil War, and to this day, dogs remain man's best friend.

A love of books links generations of our family. My path to literacy can be traced back to my mother, Amy. This book is dedicated to her, and to my Fab Five, a handful of grandchildren who can't keep their noses out of books either. "Page On," Miles, Reed, Avery, Phoebe and Parker.
—C.S.

The art is dedicated to brave Strider and the Canine Collective of Picnic Island and Circle Lake, and all the splendid dogs who give us their excellent company.
—R.B.

Reedy Press
PO Box 5131
St. Louis, MO 63139
www.reedypress.com

Library of Congress Control Number: 2013942815

ISBN: 978-1-935806-51-6

Printed in the United States of America

13 14 15 16 17   5 4 3 2 1

Seasons

Rhymes in Time

Words and Music by: Michael DeWall and Peter Elman

Illustrations by: Sara Kahn

Chillin'
Crow
Books

Chillin' Crow Books
5378 Boyd Avenue
Oakland, CA 94618

Elman, Peter 1951-, DeWall, Michael 1948-, Kahn, Sara 1965-
Seasons Rhymes In Time / Peter Elman, Michael DeWall
Illustrations and Design by Sara Kahn.
32 pages

Summary: Nine original songs with illustrations,
sheet music and accompanying CD that tell
the story of the four seasons, in nature, in rhyme.
ISBN (hardcover) 978-0-9857711-0-2.

Seasons

Rhymes in Time

Changes

Leaves are gently falling down
Morning dew is all around town
Cool days returning, clouds on the run
I've got a yearning to walk in the sun

Changes, changes, another day goes by
Changes, changes, another crimson sky

Dark outside it's getting cold
Firelight inside warms the heart and soul
Days getting shorter, rain on the way
Snow on the mountains, skies are gray

Changes, changes, another day goes by
Changes, changes, another cloudy sky

Clear blue mornings fill the sky
And the geese are flying high, goodbye
Days getting longer, perfume's in the air
In all creation here and there are

Changes, changes, another day goes by
Changes, changes, another sunny sky

Early morning at sunrise
Grandmas dream of making pies, oh my!
Berries for picking, plums on the ground
Cherries are ripe, peaches abound

Changes, changes, another day goes by
Changes, changes, another clear blue sky
Changes, changes, another year goes by
Changes, changes, another changing sky

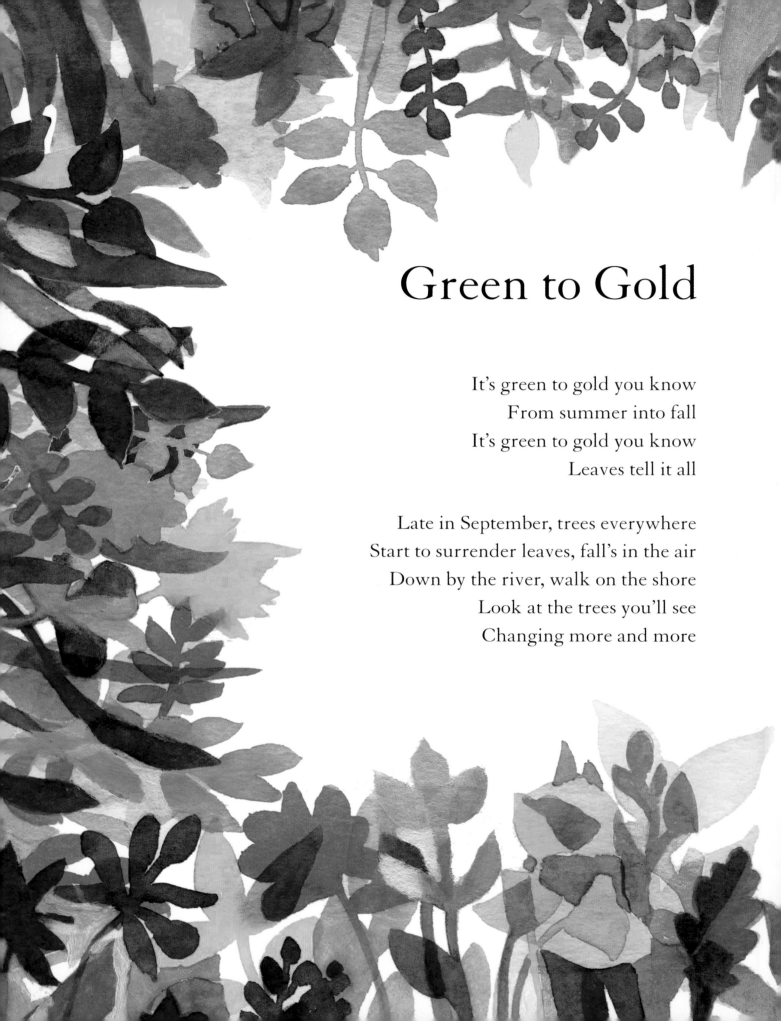

Green to Gold

It's green to gold you know
From summer into fall
It's green to gold you know
Leaves tell it all

Late in September, trees everywhere
Start to surrender leaves, fall's in the air
Down by the river, walk on the shore
Look at the trees you'll see
Changing more and more

It's green to gold you know
We're falling into fall
It's green to gold you know
Leaves tell it all

Late in October, trees getting bare
Red, yellow, green and gold, falling everywhere
Take a walk in the country, feel a breeze going by
Leaves rustling on the ground, whisper by my side

It's green to gold you know
We're heading out of fall
It's green to gold you know
Leaves tell it all

I Love Fall

I stepped outside and saw a squirrel
Running up a tree
He had an acorn in his mouth
For all the world to see

Another squirrel came running
Chased him 'round the trunk
The first one dropped that acorn
The other one had lunch

I love fall, fall, fall
It'll be September soon
Fall, fall, fall, under a harvest moon

Grandpa's got some apple trees
Growing in the back
Some are red, some are gold
Eat them for a snack

Cook them up for applesauce
Or bake them in a pie
Serve it up a la mode
My oh my

I love fall, fall, fall
On a crisp October sky
Fall, fall, fall, singing my cares away

Walking through the neighborhood
I stopped at Jones' fence
There were pumpkins everywhere
Just for fifty cents

Got my little wagon full
Pumpkins big and small
Don't you love it, Halloween
Jack o' lanterns call

I love fall, fall, fall
Underneath November's moon
Fall, fall, fall, fall most of all

Somewhere
It's Snowing

Somewhere it's snowing
A chilly wind's a-blowing
And the fire's growing warm

Somewhere the moonlight
Shines upon a cold night
And the fire's growing warm

Fall has come and gone
Ready for a winter song
There's cold in the air

Short days, longer nights
Shadows dance in pale moonlight
Dark winter is here

Snowflakes
Quiet nights
All the lakes
Have turned to ice
There's peace in the air

Footprints in the snow
Laughter echoes as we go
Under starlit skies

Sunshine's here today
The last snowman melts away
Streams singing again

Warm days, starry nights
Blue skies, not a cloud in sight
Soon winter will end

Lady Winter

Lady Winter arrives on a cloud
She finds that autumn's gone
Bare trees all around

Lady Winter lays down her first snow
It's soft and white
That's her way to say hello

When she walks there's a chill in the air
When she laughs, frost everywhere
When the winter winds blow
And the nights are aglow with her song

Lady Winter sings of winters past
Weaves her magic spell once again
But it won't last

When she walks there's a chill in the air
When she laughs, wind everywhere
When the storms get so strong
And the nights are so long, hear her song

Lady Winter has to say goodbye
Green on the trees, a breeze
A tear in her eye

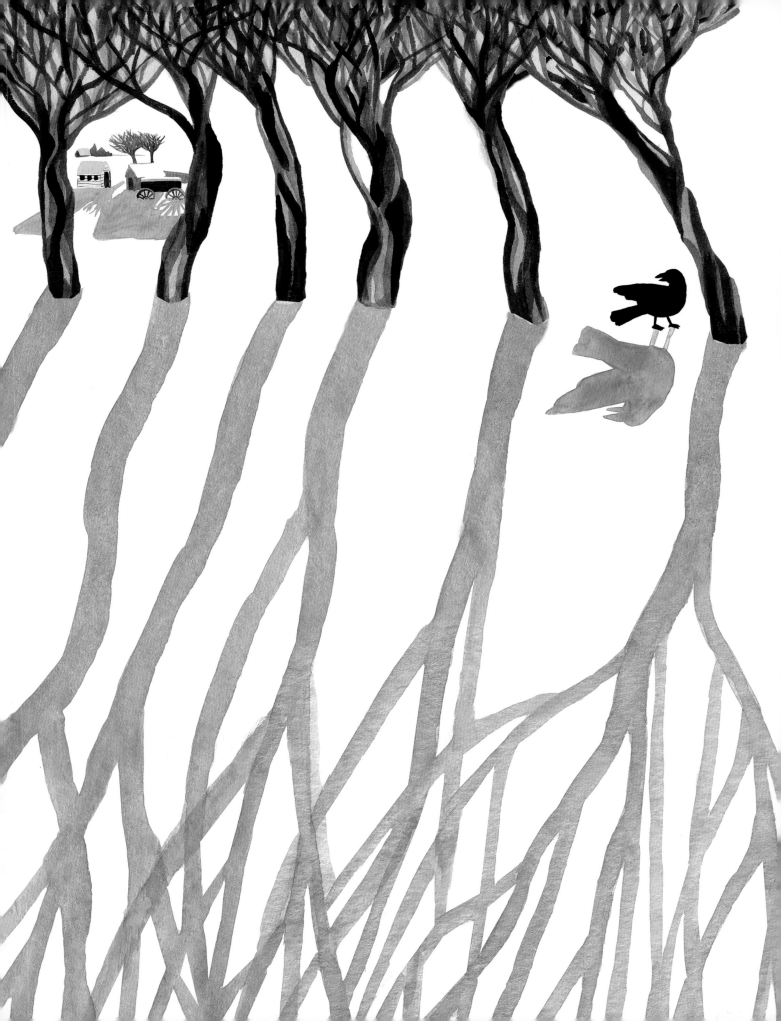

Raining

Raining, more and more
Raining, down it pours
Sitting in my room, already noon
And it won't, no it won't stop

Raining, it's coming down strong
It's been raining all day long
Sitting on my couch, I want to go out
But it won't, no it won't stop raining

Wake up don't feel sorry for yourself
Take a little walk in the rain
Get out take a look all around
Don't let the clouds get you down

Now I'm walking, there's a puddle over there
I'll get wet but I don't care
Jumping up and down, splashing all around
It's okay, you can play when it's raining

Look up, feel the rain on your face
Smile at the clouds rolling by
Raindrops such a beautiful sound
Don't let the clouds get you down

Raining, getting late
It's still raining it's almost eight
Had a lot of fun, never missed the sun
And now, it's like wow, when it's raining

Spring Song

Ribbons in hair, dancing on air
Daisy chains in May
Giggling girls full of curls
On a sunny day

I see white butterflies
I see kittens jump high
Petals arrive, bees stopping by
Spring is in the air

Short sleeve shirts play in the dirt
Sneezing everywhere
Bugs on the ground crawling around
Boys don't really care

I see puppies not dogs
I see tadpoles not frogs
Robins are out singing about
Spring is on its way

Starting a garden, I beg your pardon
Help me plant some seeds
Here come the showers, soon we'll have flowers
Help me pull some weeds

I see birds flying by
I see clouds way up high
Kites on a string doing their thing
Spring is here to stay

Picking Berries

Picking berries, making jam
Is the summer thing I love most
I put it on my pancakes
A little bit on my toast

Go for a walk in the woods, pail in your hand
Pick some and eat some the best in the land
Some of them will be sour, most of them sweet
Put them all together they make quite a treat

Picking berries, making jam
Is the summer thing I love most
I put it on my waffles
A little bit on my toast

Blueberries, raspberries, strawberries too
Any one you find that berry will do
Clean them up and cook them up in a great big old pot
With honey or sugar, and make quite a lot

Picking berries, making jam
Is the summer thing I love most
I put it on my PB&J
A little bit on my toast

Put the jam in little jars screw on a top
Put a label and a date on it, look what you got
Little jars of jam stacked on a shelf
Give some away, save some for yourself

Picking berries, making jam
Is the summer thing I love most
Remember when you pick them
They'll end up on your toast

Picking berries, making jam
Next summer let's do it again
Don't worry about getting a tummy ache
Just eat them when you can

Warm Summer Night

When the moon is shining
And the stars are bright
And the hills are glowing
On a warm summer night

When the crickets are singing
And the night owl gives a hoot
And the fireflies are glowing
When we walk, when we talk, me and you

We're at the end of a long day
Walking our troubles away
Step into the glory of nighttime
Tell me a story and then

When the warm breeze is blowing
And the leaves play their song
And the evening is calling
Come on out, sing along

When our day is over
And twilight descends
And the evening's upon us
That's when night and moonlight become friends

Notes...

Changes

Leaves are gent-ly fall-ing down.

Morn-ing dew is all a-round town.

Cool days re-turn-ing, clouds on the run.

I've got a yearn-ing to walk in the sun.

Chan-ges, chan-ges, a-no-ther day goes by.

Chan-ges, chan-ges, a-no-ther crim-son sky.

Green to Gold

It's green to gold you know from sum-mer in-to fall.

It's green to gold you know

leaves tell it all. Late in Sep-tem-

-ber, trees ev'-ry-where

start to sur-ren-der leaves, fall's in the air.

Down by the ri-ver

walk on the shore, look at the trees

you'll see chang-ing more and more.

I Love Fall

Stepped out-side and saw a squirrel run-nin' up a tree, he had an a-corn in his mouth for all the world to see. A-noth-er squirrel came run-nin', chased him 'round the trunk, the first one dropped that a-corn the o-ther one had lunch. I love fall fall fall,___ it'll be Sep-tem-ber soon, fall fall fall,___ un-der a har-vest moon.

Somewhere It's Snowing

Some-where it's snow - ing, a chil-ly wind's a - blow - ing

and the fire's grow - ing warm.

Some-where the moon - light shines up-on a cold night

and the fire's grow - ing warm.

Fall has come and gone, rea - dy for a win - ter song,

there's cold in the air.

Short days long-er nights, sha-dows dance in pale moon-light,

dark win - ter is here.

Lady Winter

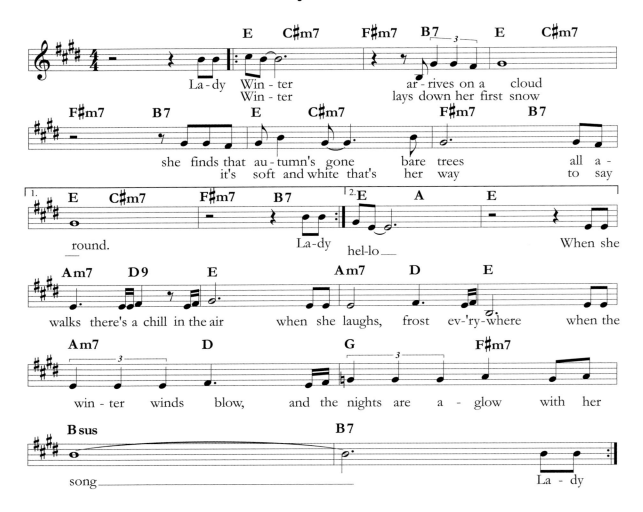

E C#m7 F#m7 B7   E C#m7

La - dy Win - ter ar - rives on a cloud
Win - ter lays down her first snow

F#m7 B7   E C#m7   F#m7 B7

she finds that au - tumn's gone bare trees all a -
it's soft and white that's her way to say

1. E C#m7 F#m7 B7 2. E A E

round.   La-dy hel-lo When she

Am7 D9 E   Am7 D E

walks there's a chill in the air when she laughs, frost ev-'ry-where when the

Am7 D   G   F#m7

win - ter winds blow, and the nights are a - glow with her

B sus   B7

song   La - dy

Raining

Rain-in' more and more, rain-in' down it pours,

sit-tin' in my room, al-rea-dy noon and it won't, no it won't stop.

Rain-in', com-in' down strong it's been rain-in' all day long,

sit-tin' on my couch I wan-na go out but it won't, no it won't stop

rain-in'. Wake up don't feel sor-ry for your-self,

take a lit-tle walk in the rain. Get out take a look all a-round,

don't let the clouds get you down.

Spring Song

Rib-bons in hair dan-cing on air,

dai - sy chains in May.

Gig - gling girls full of curls,

on a sun - ny day.

I see white but - ter - flies,

I see kit - tens jump high.

Pet - als ar - rive, bees stop-ping by,

spring is in the air.

3X

Picking Berries

Pick - in' ber - ries mak - in' jam,_____ is the
sum - mer thing_____ I love most._____ I
put it on my pan - cakes_____ a
lit - tle bit on my toast.

Go for a walk in the woods, pail in your hand
pick some and eat some the best in the land.

Some of 'em 'll be so - ur, most of them sweet,
put 'em all to - ge - ther they make quite a treat.

Warm Summer Night

When the moon is shin - ing and the stars are bright, and the hills are glow - in' on a warm sum - mer night. When the crick-ets are sing - in' and the night owl gives a hoot, and the fire - flies are glow - in' when we walk when we talk me and you. We're at the end of a long day walk - in' our trou-bles a-way. Step in-to the glo - ry of night - time, tell me a sto - ry and then. When the

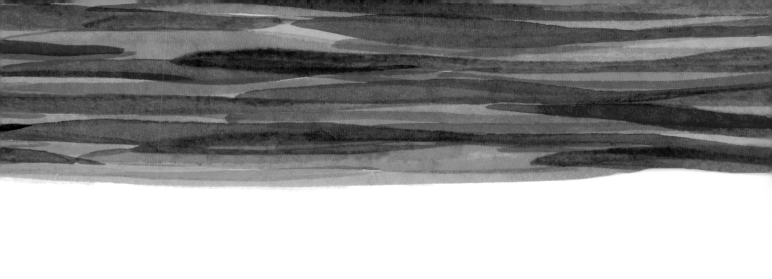

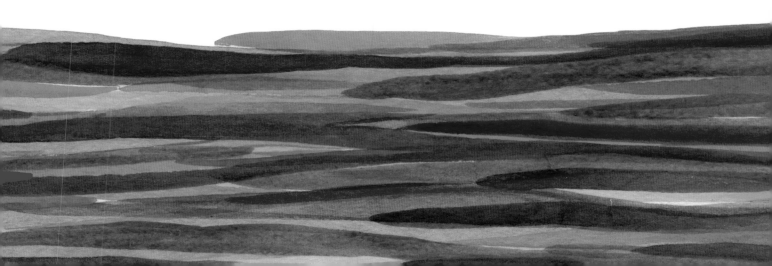